# Karen's Tea Party

**Look for these
and other books about Karen
in the
Baby-sitters Little Sister series:**

# Little Sister

# Karen's Tea Party

## Ann M. Martin

Illustrations by Susan Tang

A
**LITTLE APPLE**
PAPERBACK

SCHOLASTIC INC.
New York Toronto London Auckland Sydney

No part of this publication may be reproduced in whole or in part, or stored in a retrieval system, or transmitted in any form or by any means, electronic, mechanical, photocopying, recording, or otherwise, without written permission of the publisher. For information regarding permission, write to Scholastic Inc., 730 Broadway, New York, NY 10003.

ISBN 0-590-44828-5

12 11                                                                9/9 0/0

Printed in the U.S.A.                                            40

First Scholastic printing, May 1992

*The author gratefully acknowledges*
*Stephanie Calmenson*
*for her help*
*with this book.*

# The Rice Mess

"We're here!" I called. "We're here!"

Where were we? At the big house. That's what we call my daddy's house. It was late Friday afternoon and Mommy had just dropped us off.

Who are we? I am Karen Brewer. I am seven years old. I have blonde hair, blue eyes, and some freckles. Oh, yes, I wear glasses. Andrew is my little brother. He is almost five. He looks a lot like me. But he does not wear glasses.

Daddy came to the door and gave us big hugs.

"Where is everyone?" I asked.

"We thought it would be fun to make dinner together tonight. Everyone is inside," answered Daddy.

I dropped my knapsack and raced into the kitchen. I didn't want anything fun to happen without me.

"I want to help! I want to help!" I said.

"Hi, Karen," said Kristy. "You can help me make the salad." (Kristy is my big stepsister and one of my favorite people in the whole world.)

"Thanks," I said. "But I want to make something by myself."

"We are having chicken, rice, and salad," said Elizabeth. "I don't think anyone's making the rice yet. Would you like to do that?"

"Sure!" I replied. The rice was the second most important part of dinner. I felt gigundoly important.

"You can make the rice by yourself," said

Daddy. "But one of us will watch you when you are at the stove."

"Uh-oh. Karen is cooking. No rice for dinner tonight," teased my stepbrother, Sam.

"Just wait. I am going to make the best rice ever," I said.

I found the box of rice. The directions were on the back:

*Step 1: Bring four cups of water to a boil.* I learned in school that when water boils you can see big bubbles. I poured the water into a pot. Daddy watched me turn on the stove. Then I waited and waited. I watched and watched. No bubbles. I could not wait forever. So when the water looked hot enough to me, I went to the next step.

*Step 2: Add 2 cups of rice, 2 tbsps. of butter, and 2 tsps. of salt.* Hmm. This recipe had secret codes. What did *tbsps.* and *tsps.* mean? No problem. I measured 2 cups of rice. Then I added a stick of butter and half a shaker of salt. This rice was going to be delicious!

*Step 3: Cover tightly and simmer over low heat about 20 minutes.* I never heard the word *simmer* before. But it sounded a lot like *swimmer*. I decided that meant you should let the rice swim around awhile. So I did.

*Step 4: Let rice stand 1 minute until it is fluffy and dry.* "Okay, rice," I said. "Stand right where you are. Do not sit down." I thought that was pretty funny. Then I waited for one minute, and called, "The rice is ready!"

"Karen, are you sure?" asked Elizabeth. "That seemed awfully fast."

"I'm a fast cooker!" I replied.

I picked up the lid of the pot. "Ta-da!" I said proudly.

What a mess! The rice was not fluffy and dry. Half of it was stuck to the bottom of the pot. The rest was floating at the top.

I was so, so mad. I picked up the box of rice and shook it. Rice went flying everywhere.

"Who writes these directions anyway?" I said. "There are secret codes and words you cannot even understand. I am going upstairs right now to write a letter to the rice company. They will be sorry!"

I left my big house family standing in the kitchen with their mouths hanging open.

# After the Divorce

I picked up my purple pen and my pink paper and started to write:

*Dear Rice Company,*

*I am sitting upstairs in my room at the big house and I am writing to tell you . . .*

Wait, I thought. Maybe I should tell them about the big house. And the little house, too. You see, I live in two houses. This is why.

A long time ago Mommy and Daddy decided they didn't love each other anymore. So they got divorced. We had been living at the big house here in Stoneybrook, Connecticut. (The big house is the house Daddy grew up in.) But after the divorce, Mommy moved out with Andrew and me.

We moved into a little house. (It is in Stoneybrook, Connecticut, too.) Then Mommy got married again to a man named Seth. He is my stepfather. Seth is very nice. He moved into the little house with us. He brought along his dog Midgie, and his cat Rocky. (I guess they are my step-pets.) So now Mommy, Andrew, Seth, Midgie, Rocky, Emily Junior (she's my pet rat), and I live together in the little house most of the time.

But every other weekend, and on some holidays, and for two weeks in the summer, Andrew and I go to the big house, where Daddy still lives.

After the divorce, Daddy got married again, too. He married Elizabeth. Now she's my stepmother. She moved into the big house with her four children. They are Sam and Charlie (they're in high school),

David Michael (he's seven, like me), and Kristy (she's thirteen).

Then Daddy and Elizabeth adopted Emily Michelle from a faraway place called Vietnam. She's two and a half. I named my rat after her. Nannie, Elizabeth's mother (my stepgrandmother), moved into the big house after Emily Michelle came. Nannie takes care of Emily Michelle when the rest of the family are at work or at school.

I almost forgot to tell you about the pets at the big house. David Michael has a Bernese mountain dog puppy named Shannon. Daddy has a fat tiger cat named Boo-Boo. Andrew has a fish named Goldfishie. And I have a fish named Crystal Light the Second. (That is because Crystal Light the First died.)

So Andrew and I have two families, two houses, two sets of pets, and two of lots of other things. For example, I have two stuffed cats. Moosie stays at the big house. Goosie stays at the little house. And I have two pieces of my special blanket, Tickly. (I had to cut Tickly in half because I kept leaving him behind at one house or the other, and I need him with me to go to sleep.)

I even have two best friends. Nancy Dawes lives next door to Mommy. Hannie Papadakis lives across the street and one house over from Daddy. Nancy and Hannie and I call ourselves the Three Musketeers.

Do you know what I call myself? Karen Two-Two! And I call my brother Andrew Two-Two. (I got that name from a book my teacher, Ms. Colman, read at school. It was called *Jacob Two-Two Meets the Hooded Fang*.)

So that is the story of the big house and the little house. I tried to decide if the rice company would be interested.

"Karen! Dinner is ready!" called Kristy.

Thank goodness! I was gigundoly hungry. I wondered what we were going to have instead of rice. I hurried downstairs to find out.

# The Goops

Spaghetti. Thanks to Nannie, that is what we had instead of rice.

We ate together in the kitchen. It is a lot less fancy than the big house dining room.

"Please pass the pasketti," I said. (That is what Andrew calls spaghetti.)

I was secretly glad we were having spaghetti instead of rice. Spaghetti is more fun. I found a really long piece in my dish. I held it up over my mouth. Then I sucked it in with one slurp.

10

"Karen, no slurping, please," said Daddy.

"Sorry," I said.

*Blub, blub, blub. Blub, blub, blub.*

Andrew was blowing bubbles in his milk.

"Andrew, no bubbles," said Daddy.

Suddenly we heard a sound that was like an elephant trumpeting in the jungle. I didn't even know where the sound was coming from. But Elizabeth did.

"David Michael, please stop making that noise with your armpit. It is very rude," she said.

I thought it was very funny. And I wanted to add to the noise. So I took a big swallow of air and tried to burp. Sam showed me how to do it once.

I ended up choking and coughing instead.

"Try again," whispered Sam. "Bring the air way down and push it up again. Like this. . . ." *Urrrrp!*

"Sam!" said Daddy. "It is one thing for the younger children to forget their table

manners. But you're in high school."

"Sorry," said Sam.

"I think we'd better eat a little more quietly," suggested Elizabeth. "No slurping, burping, bubble blowing, or making animal noises for the rest of the meal."

"I agree," said Daddy. "Some people at this table are rather ill-mannered. In fact, they are behaving like the Goops."

"Who are the Goops?" I asked.

Elizabeth smiled. "There's a book called *Goop Tales* by a man named Gilett Burgess," she said. "It tells everything you could ever want to know about the Goops. I have an old copy somewhere. I'll look for it after dinner."

We tried to eat more quietly after that. *Blub, blub. Urrrp!* I guess we did not do a very good job.

When we finished eating, David Michael, Andrew, and I went into the den. We drew pictures of what we thought the Goops would look like. In the meantime, Elizabeth searched for her book.

"I found it!" she called.

Elizabeth read us a story about the Goop Family at dinner. They blew bubbles in their water, made strange noises, and squirted whipped cream all over the table. They really did sound like us. Especially a little Goop girl named Quirita. Elizabeth read us a poem about her. This is how it went:

She has a Funny Name — QUIRITA!
Yet Never Little Girl was Sweeter.
So Seldom was she Found to Blame
You'll Wonder How she Got her Name —
But if you Dined with her, you'd Know;
Her Table Manners, they were Low!

Andrew and I could hardly stop laughing. "Get it?" I said. "Quirita? A queer eater?" We thought the Goops were very funny.

"Are you a Goop?" I asked Andrew.

"Yup!" said Andrew. "Are you?"

"Yup!" I said.

"I don't like all this talk about manners," said David Michael.

He looked worried. I began to wonder why.

# Mr. Peabody's School of Dance and Charm

"Red light, green light, one, two, three!" I shouted. I turned around. Everyone was frozen in place. Boo. I wanted my friends to move so I could send them back to the starting line.

It was late Saturday morning. I was in the big house backyard with Andrew, David Michael, Hannie, Linny (Hannie's brother), and Melody and Bill Korman (our new neighbors).

"*Achoo!*" sneezed David Michael.

"You moved. You have to go back to the starting line!" I said.

"That is not fair. Sneezing does not count," said David Michael.

"Does too," I said.

"Does not," said David Michael.

"Doesn't matter," called Charlie, sticking his head out the back door. "The game is over. Time for lunch."

"See you later!" I said to my friends. "We have to go inside now."

We raced to the kitchen. That is because Saturday lunches at the big house are the most fun. Daddy and Elizabeth practically empty out the refrigerator and food shelves. They put everything on the kitchen table and let us pick whatever we want.

My Saturday lunch used to be peanut butter on celery sticks. But now I eat a peanut butter and banana sandwich, just like Kristy. And I have an apple, potato chips, and milk. Yum!

I was having a little trouble eating. That is because I was still out of breath from running. And my hands were sweaty and slippery, so my apple kept sliding around. And I was trying to eat around the dirty fingerprints on my sandwich.

*Urrrp!* "That was a good one," said David Michael. "I bet you cannot burp so loud, Karen."

"I bet I can. I have been practicing since last night," I said. I took a deep swallow of air.

*Urrr-urr-urrp!*

"Now that is what I call a burp!" said Sam.

"I have an announcement to make," said Daddy.

"Is it a Surprising Announcement?" I asked. (At school, Ms. Colman makes Surprising Announcements. They are almost always something great.)

"Yes, I think you will be surprised," said Daddy. "I have enrolled you and David Michael in Mr. Peabody's School of Dance and Charm. You will learn some ballroom dancing. And you will learn some manners."

"Cool! Gigundo cool!" I said. "Amanda Delaney went to Mr. Peabody's school, too."

Amanda was my friend who used to live two houses over from Hannie. Then she moved away. Melody and Bill Korman live in her house now.

When Amanda went to Mr. Peabody's, she got to buy a fancy dress. And one day a week she got to act like a grand lady.

"It will be just like playing our Lovely Ladies game," I said to Kristy. Amanda taught me to play that. We get all dressed up and say, "Oh, I am a lovely, lovely lady."

"Well, I'm not going to be a lovely lady! No way," said David Michael.

"There will be other boys there," said Elizabeth.

"I don't care. I am not going to some silly

*charming* school," said David Michael. He sounded like he meant it.

But I could tell Daddy meant it more when he said, "Your mother and I have decided you are going, David Michael. And that is final."

# Ribbons and Bows

"*Oh, I want to be a lovely, lovely lady. That is what I truly want to be!*"

It was Saturday morning at the little house. I was sitting in front of my mirror. I was singing a lovely lady song to the tune of my favorite hot dog commercial.

"Elizabeth and Kristy will be here any minute, Karen. Are you ready to go?" called Mommy.

"Yes! I will be right down," I answered.

Even though it was a little house week-end, Elizabeth and Kristy were taking me shopping. That is because Monday was my first day at Mr. Peabody's school. I already had party shoes. But I needed a fancy new dress. And white gloves. (Elizabeth volunteered to take me shopping because Mr. Peabody's school was her and Daddy's idea.)

*Beep! Beep!*

"Be good," said Mommy. She waved good-bye to me and Elizabeth and Kristy as we headed into town.

"We will try Madame Drew's Dress Shop first," said Elizabeth.

We found a parking spot right in front of the store.

"Look at the dress in the window!" I cried.

It was gigundoly beautiful. It was white with tiny pink and blue flowers all over. The sleeves were puffy with ribbons tied around them. And at the waist was a big pink bow. I *love* ribbons and bows!

"Let's see if they have your size," said Elizabeth.

22

"May I help you?" asked the saleswoman.

"Yes, thank you," said Elizabeth. "This is Karen, and she needs a new dress for Mr. Peabody's school."

"Hello, Karen," said the woman. "My name is Mrs. Oliver. I am sure we will have something you like."

"I like the dress in the window," I said.

"I will see if we have it in your size," said Mrs. Oliver. "Please have a seat."

I sank into a big red armchair. This was nothing like the stores I went to for my jeans and sneakers.

When Mrs. Oliver came back, her arms were filled with dresses. Pink dresses, white dresses, velvet dresses. Wow!

I tried them all. I liked them. But something was missing from every one.

"Wait," I said. "The one from the window is not here."

"I'm afraid I did not see that one in your size," said Mrs. Oliver.

**5** *Madame Drew's Dress Shop*

"But I like it the best. It is the fanciest!" I cried.

"These dresses are pretty, too," said Kristy.

"The one in the window looked like it would fit me. Can you see if it is my size? Please? Puh-lease?" I begged.

"I'll go look," said Mrs. Oliver.

After awhile, Mrs. Oliver came back carrying the dress from the window.

"You were right," she said. "It is your size."

"Thank you!" I cried.

I put on the dress. It was my absolute, number one, very special favorite.

"We'll take it," said Elizabeth.

Mrs. Oliver wrapped up my dress in a fancy box. I felt gigundoly special carrying it outside. I saw Mrs. Oliver putting a new dress in the window. It wasn't half as nice as mine.

"Our next stop is Bellair's Department Store," said Elizabeth as we climbed into the car.

I went into Bellair's empty-handed. But I came out carrying two bags. One held my new white gloves. The other held my fancy new hair clip with shiny white pearls.

I was so excited. I could not stop singing the whole way home.

*"Oh, I am going to be a lovely, lovely lady. When Monday comes, everyone will see!"*

# The Cookie Mess

"Goosie, may I have this dance?" I asked.

I held Goosie up to my ear and listened for his answer.

"You would be delighted, but you need me to lead? I would be glad to," I said.

I took Goosie in my arms and began to hum. *Hum-de-hum-hum. Hum-de-hum.* I twirled around and around the room. I twirled so much, I made myself dizzy. I had to sit down.

"Thank you for the dance, Goosie," I said, holding my head in my hands.

It was Sunday morning. One and a half days to Mr. Peabody's school. I looked at my dress hanging on my door. I looked at the new white gloves and pearl hair clip on my dresser. I was ready for a party and dancing. I could not wait until Monday. I had to do something fancy now.

I knew just the thing. I ran downstairs to ask Mommy. I was so excited, I could not stop talking.

"Mommy, may I use the phone? I want to call Nancy. I want to invite her to a tea party. May I have a tea party? I want it to be very special. I want to make cookies. Do we have chocolate chips? I will make chocolate chippies!"

"Whoa, Karen. You better slow down or you will be too tired to make anything," said Mommy. "Here are the answers to your questions. Yes, you may use the phone. Yes, you may have a tea party.

And yes, we have chocolate chips."

"Hurray!" I cried. I called Nancy. She said she would come over at three.

I invited Andrew, Goosie, Rocky, Midgie, and Hyacynthia, the special English baby doll that I share with Nancy. They all said they could come.

Mommy was in the kitchen. She was getting out everything I needed to bake cookies.

"Thanks, Mommy. But I want to make the cookies by myself," I announced.

"I guess that will be all right," agreed Mommy. "But I must be in the kitchen when you use the oven."

"I promise to call when I need you," I said, shooing Mommy out the door.

I picked up the bag of chocolate chips. Just as I had hoped, the directions were on the back. I was sure they would be better than the directions on the rice box. (Someday I would finish that letter to the rice company.)

The first thing I had to do was preheat the oven to 375 degrees.

"Mommy, I need you!" I called. Mommy came back to turn on the oven. Then I shooed her out again.

The rest looked easy. I had to mix together butter, sugar, eggs, vanilla, flour, salt, baking soda, and chocolate chips. There were no hard words. And there were no secret codes.

It took awhile, but I put everything in exactly the way the package said. Then I did one special thing. I squirted in some liquid brown sugar. That way my tea party cookies would be extra sweet.

I was ready to spoon the batter onto the cookie sheet. Hmm. The batter looked a little soupy. The chocolate chips stayed where they were, but everything else ran together. It was cookie soup!

"Mommy! I need you," I called.

Mommy came back into the kitchen.

"Yes?" she said.

"Would you turn the oven off, please? I

have decided to serve milk and crackers at my party," I explained.

Mommy looked at the baking sheet. It was a runny cookie mess.

"I think crackers are a good idea," said Mommy. And she turned the oven off.

# "No Burping Allowed!"

"Will you button up my dress, Mommy?" I asked.

"Will you fix my tie?" asked Andrew.

We were almost ready for my tea party. Mommy let me wear my new dress and hair clip. (I decided to save my gloves for my first day at Mr. Peabody's.)

It wasn't easy, but I got Andrew to put on a suit and tie. (He said I owed him a big favor now. He even made me write it down on a piece of paper so I would not forget.)

33

*Ding-dong.*

"I will get it!" I called.

It was Nancy. She looked beautiful. Almost as beautiful as me. She was wearing a light blue dress with a matching hair ribbon. She was carrying a white pocketbook with blue polka dots. She was also carrying something wrapped in pretty paper.

"Hi, Karen. This is for you," said Nancy.

I opened the package. It was a jar of grape jelly.

"Thank you so much," I said in my most lovely lady voice. "This will be quite tasty on our crackers."

I hurried Nancy into the kitchen. I could hardly wait for her to see the table I had set.

My best flowery tea set was at the big house. But Mommy said I could use some of her old china. It was chipped but very pretty. And at every place was a Pooh Bear napkin.

My other guests looked great, too. Hyacynthia was wearing the beaded necklace

Nancy had made for her. Goosie was wearing one of Andrew's ties. Midgie was wearing a red scarf. I even put a party hat on Rocky.

"Andrew! We are ready," I called. I could not figure out what he was up to. He had spent half the morning in his room with the door closed. He said he was practicing something. But he would not tell me what it was.

Finally, Andrew came downstairs.

"Hi. Where's the duck food?" he said.

"What duck food? This is a tea party," I said.

"I thought you were having *quackers* and milk. Get it? Crackers? Quackers?" Andrew was slapping the table and laughing.

Nancy was laughing, too. Didn't they know this was a serious tea party?

Then I brought out the milk and crackers and jelly.

Midgie tried to steal a cracker. Rocky jumped on the table and almost spilled the milk.

"Where are your manners?" I said. I asked them both to leave the party.

Everything was going nicely after that until . . .

*Urrrrp!*

"I did it!" cried Andrew. "I burped on purpose."

"Is that what you were practicing upstairs?" I said.

"Yup," said Andrew proudly. "Sam taught me."

For some reason, Nancy thought this was hysterical.

"No burping allowed," I said. "And no laughing at burping, either."

"Sorry," said Nancy. "Would you pass the — "

*Urrrp!*

"An-drew!" I shouted.

"I have to practice or I will forget," said Andrew.

Nancy was laughing so hard she tipped her chair back and fell over. I could tell she was not hurt.

"I said no burping. And no tipping over chairs! Doesn't anybody around here have any manners?"

"We are just having fun," said Nancy.

"You can have fun and good manners, too," I said.

"I am going to Mr. Peabody's school next year. I will have better manners then," said Nancy.

"Well, I cannot wait that long," I said. "I am starting Mr. Peabody's school tomorrow. I am going to teach you everything I know. And you, too, Andrew."

*Urrrp!*

# The School of Charm

"See you later, Mommy!" I called. I swished up the steps of Mr. Peabody's School of Dance and Charm in my beautiful new dress.

"Hi, Karen," said a familiar voice.

It was Ricky Torres. Ricky is my pretend husband. We got married once at school. He is a pretty good husband — most of the time.

"This is so cool," I said. "I did not know you were signed up for Mr. Peabody's."

"A lot of kids from our class are here," said Ricky.

I looked around. The room was huge and filled with kids. I saw David Michael. He did not look happy.

I waved to Hannie and her brother, Linny. And Scott Hsu. He is Hannie's pretend husband. I knew both of them would be here.

But I did not know Natalie Springer had signed up. Or Hank Reubens. Or Bobby Gianelli. They are in my class, too.

Yuck-o! Pamela Harding and her friends Leslie Morris and Jannie Gilbert walked in. Pamela is my least favorite person at school.

"Welcome, everyone," said a man standing by a piano. "I am Mr. Peabody. And these are my assistants — my lovely wife, Mrs. Peabody, and my son, Martin."

The Peabodys were all dressed up like the rest of us. Even Martin, who looked about Kristy's age.

"We will begin our class by teaching the

boys how to invite a girl to dance," said Mr. Peabody.

All of a sudden, the boys were moving. Backwards. Away from the girls.

"It is really very simple," continued Mr. Peabody. "Walk up to a girl, look in her eyes, and say, 'May I have this dance?' "

"Girls, the polite answer is, 'Yes, you may,' " said Mrs. Peabody.

"While you are dancing, compliment your partner," said Mr. Peabody. "Say, 'My, you are a good dancer.' "

"To accept a compliment, just say, 'Thank you,' " added Mrs. Peabody.

I raised my hand and called, "I thought you were supposed to say, 'Charmed, I'm sure.' "

"A simple thank you will do," said Mr. Peabody. "Now we will begin with a dance called the lindy. Martin will play the piano for us. Martin?"

Martin bowed and started to play. I liked the music. It made me want to dance. I just had to learn how.

"Sway your body forward and back, like this," said Mr. Peabody. "Now, watch my feet. Toe, heel. Toe, heel. Step. Step."

I was in the front with Natalie and Hannie and some girls I did not know. We were following Mr. and Mrs. Peabody. Toe, heel. Toe, heel. Step. Step.

A few boys were dancing. But most of them looked like they were glued to the wall. Didn't they know this was fun?

We practiced by ourselves for awhile. Then Mr. Peabody said. "Boys, it is time to ask a girl to dance."

I knew Ricky would ask me. But he was not exactly running to me. And when he reached me, he talked so low and so fast, I could hardly understand him. It sounded like he said, "Maythisdance?"

"Charmed, I'm sure," I replied. (I liked that even if Mr. Peabody didn't.)

I put one hand on Ricky's shoulder. He put one hand on my waist. (I could tell he did not want to.) We held our other hands.

(His was cold and sweaty. I could feel it even through my glove.)

We started to dance. Toe, heel. Toe, heel. Step. Step. Toe, heel. Toe, heel. Step. Step.

Most of the girls were bouncing and swaying, like me. Most of the boys were staring at the ground and grumbling, like Ricky. I wished he would try to have some fun.

Oh, well. I loved the lindy. And I loved Mr. Peabody's School of Dance and Charm even if Ricky Torres did not. I could hardly wait for my next lesson.

9

# "May I Have This Dance?"

Toe, heel. Toe, heel. Step. Step.

I was at the back of Ms. Colman's room practicing the lindy with Hannie and Natalie. Nancy was at the end of our line, trying to follow us. Pamela and Leslie were practicing at the other side of the room.

Ms. Colman had not come in yet, so I turned to Hannie and said, "May I have this dance?"

"Yes, you may," said Hannie, just the way Mr. and Mrs. Peabody had taught us.

I curtsied. Hannie bowed. (I did not

know whether you were supposed to do that for a lindy. But we did it anyway.)

We needed some music, so I made up a tune.

*"Da-da, da-da, da-da-da! Da-da, da-da, da!"* I sang.

We danced around the room and between the desks. It was gigundoly fun! Until the boys started saying dumb things.

"Toe, heel. Big deal!" called Hank Reubens.

I stuck my nose in the air as I passed him.

"Toe, heel. Get real!" called Bobby Gianelli.

Then I noticed Ricky pointing at my feet. I looked down to see just what he was pointing at and missed my step. I stomped on Hannie's foot.

"Ow!" cried Hannie.

Ricky and the other boys thought that was so funny, they could hardly stop laughing.

"Didn't you learn *any*thing about manners yesterday?" I asked. I gave Ricky a dirty look. I expected more from my own husband.

"I learned some manners," said Hank. "Listen to this!"

Hank snorted like a pig. Bobby mooed like a cow. And Ricky said, "Hee-haw, hee-haw!"

"Can't these boys take anything seriously?" said Hannie.

"I don't think so," I replied. "I just hope they do not act dumb next Monday at Mr. Peabody's class. They will ruin everything."

# 10

# "May I Have These Pants?"

T.G.I.M. Thank goodness it's Monday!

I raced through the doors of Mr. Peabody's school. It probably would have been better manners to walk in slowly. But Mr. Peabody had not said so. Yet.

"Hi, Hannie! Hi, Natalie," I called.

We were on one side of the room. The boys were all the way on the other.

"Welcome, class," said Mr. Peabody. "We are going to begin with a lesson in the art of conversation. I have noticed that many of you, particularly the boys, stand away from others and do not speak."

David Michael was way over in a corner of the room. He started shuffling his feet.

"It is good manners to make pleasant conversation when in the company of others," Mr. Peabody continued. "You might start by saying, 'Hello, it is nice to see you.' Or you can begin with a compliment. Say, 'I like your dress.' Or 'I like your suit.' "

"Does anyone have another suggestion?" asked Mrs. Peabody.

I did. I raised my hand to show my good manners. Mrs. Peabody pointed to me.

"You could talk about the weather," I said. "Like you could say, 'How about that hurricane last night?' "

"Talking about the weather is very good," said Mrs. Peabody.

"And now," said Mr. Peabody, "we will review the lindy. Martin, will you play something for us?"

Martin bowed, then started to play.

I had been practicing the lindy all week long. I did not miss one step.

48

"Very good, class. We are ready to learn the waltz," said Mr. Peabody.

"Oooooh!" I said. That sounded fancy. I was glad I was wearing my fancy party dress.

"Please pay careful attention. The first step is most important," said Mr. Peabody. "*One*, two, three. *One*, two, three. *Watch* . . . my . . . feet. *Watch* . . . my . . . feet."

He took Mrs. Peabody in his arms. They danced the waltz together. It was gigundoly romantic.

"*One*, two, three. *One*, two, three," he said.

I followed his steps.

"*One*, two, three. *One*, two, three," I repeated.

"And now with music. Martin?" said Mr. Peabody.

When Martin started playing, I said, "Hey, I know this." I hummed along. It was the music they play at the skating rink.

I closed my eyes and counted. *One*, two, three. *One*, two, three.

"Now it is time to dance with a partner," said Mr. Peabody.

I was glad to see Ricky walking toward me a lot faster than he had before. But this strange smile was on his face.

"May I have these pants?" he said. He looked behind him to make sure the Peabodys did not hear.

"Ricky! That is just plain dumb," I whispered.

Hannie was next to me. I heard Scott say, "I am glad you are wearing those gloves, Hannie. Now I do not have to worry so much about girl cooties."

I wanted to say something mean. But I didn't do it. The boys could have bad manners if they wanted.

But not me.

# Karen the Teacher

"Boys! They make me so mad," I said.

"I am a boy. Do I make you mad?" asked Andrew.

"Not this minute. But I bet you will soon," I said.

"Now, Karen, that is not fair," said Mommy.

I was in the kitchen having a snack after Mr. Peabody's class.

"Mommy, can I ask Nancy to come over? I want to teach her what I learned at school. And Andrew, too," I said.

"It is all right with me if it is all right with Mrs. Dawes," said Mommy.

I called Nancy. She said she would come right over. Mommy helped me move chairs out of the way in the living room. We needed plenty of room for dancing.

*Ding-dong.*

"Hi, Karen! Hi, Andrew," said Nancy.

"Hello, Nancy," I said. "You showed very good manners when you said hello to everyone in the room. Now before we begin our dancing lesson, you and Andrew should have a pleasant conversation. You should think of a compliment to say. Or talk about the weather."

"Can't we just start dancing?" asked Nancy.

"No, we cannot. Mr. Peabody says polite conversation is very important," I said.

"Oh, all right," said Nancy. She turned to Andrew. "How is the weather?"

"Okay. I like your shoes," said Andrew.

"Thank you. Now can we start dancing?" said Nancy.

"That was a very nice conversation," I said. "We will now learn the lindy. Watch my feet."

I hummed my lindy song and did a few steps.

*Hmm-hmm, hmm-hmm, hmm, hmm!*

"Follow me," I said. "Toe, heel. Toe, heel. Step. Step. Toe, heel. Toe, heel. Step. Step. Got it?"

"Toe, heel. Heel and toe. Step. What?" asked Nancy.

"Nancy, you were *not* watching closely enough. Please try again," I said.

"I was too watching," said Nancy. "I just forgot."

"I cannot do this," moaned Andrew.

I repeated the steps very slowly.

Toe, heel. Toe, heel. Step. Step.

I kept doing it until Nancy and Andrew each did it right once.

"Time for partners!" I called. "Andrew, walk up to Nancy, look her in the eyes, and say, 'May I have this dance?' "

Andrew did it perfectly.

"Great," I told him. "Now, you put this hand on her waist here and — "

"No way. I am not touching a girl!" said Andrew.

He stomped out of the room. I threw my hands in the air.

"Can you believe that?" I said. "He is such a silly baby."

"Boys are so rude. They never cooperate," said Nancy.

"They are just awful. They will not *do* anything," I added.

"They are big spoilsports," agreed Nancy.

"Boys," I said. "They make me so mad!"

# Pig

It was Monday afternoon. I was at dance class number three.

Metal folding chairs were lined up around the room. I looked to see who had arrived. I saw Hannie. And Natalie. I saw Pamela. And Leslie. But I did not see Ricky.

That is strange, I thought. Ricky was at school today. And I was sure I saw him in the coatroom with Bobby and Hank when I first reached Mr. Peabody's. He must be here somewhere.

I was still looking for Ricky when Mr.

Peabody said, "Welcome, everyone. We are going to begin today by learning the proper way to sit."

I could not find Ricky anywhere. I did not see Bobby or Hank, either. Hmm.

"Girls, cross you ankles. Boys, keep your legs together. Everyone, fold your hands in your lap and sit up nice and tall," said Mr. Peabody.

I made sure I was sitting exactly right.

"Boys, please stand now and be ready to invite a girl to dance. Martin?" said Mr. Peabody.

Martin began playing a waltz. A boy I did not know walked over to me and said, "May I have this dance?"

"Yes, you may," I answered. (I decided to try it Mr. Peabody's way.)

*One*, two, three. *One*, two, three. This was *fun*, two, three. *Fun*, two, three.

The boy did not say anything weird like, "Keep your cooties to yourself." He was nice and po*lite*, two, three. I had to count.

I did not want to step on this nice boy's feet.

Suddenly, the music stopped. Everyone turned around to see what was happening.

"Right this way, boys," Mr. Peabody said. He did not look too happy. Neither did Ricky, Hank, or Bobby. They followed Mr. Peabody into the room.

"Will all the girls please return to your seats. Will all the boys stay where you are. We will begin the dance again," said Mrs. Peabody.

Martin began another waltz. This time, Ricky walked over to me.

"May I have this dance?" he said.

"Yes, you may," I replied. "And you better tell me what happened," I whispered.

"Bobby and Hank and I did not want to go to another dumb dance class," said Ricky. "We were hiding in the coatroom till it was over."

"How did you get caught?" I asked.

"We were playing cards," said Ricky. "Bobby was shuffling them too loudly."

"Which game?" I wanted to know.

"Pig," mumbled Ricky.

Probably Hank's idea, I thought. Boys. You cannot take them anywhere.

"What is Mr. Peabody going to do?" I whispered.

"I do not know. Tell our parents, I guess," said Ricky. "Hey! Maybe he will kick us out of dance school!"

I shook my head sadly. Boys are just hopeless.

# For Girls Only

"Can you believe it?" I said. "They were playing Pig in the coatroom."

"I bet Mr. Peabody told their parents," said Hannie.

It was Tuesday morning. We were telling Nancy about dance class while we waited for Ms. Colman.

"Those boys are so dumb," said Nancy.

"They sure are," said Terri.

Her twin sister, Tammy, agreed. Even

60

Pamela, Leslie, and Jannie thought the boys were dumb.

"They are going to be in big trouble," said Natalie. "If I were them, I would be scared." (Natalie is scared of most things.)

"Shh. Here comes Ricky," whispered Hannie.

"Hi, Ricky," I said. "What happened when you got home? Did you get in trouble?"

"Yes," admitted Ricky. "My parents are taking away my allowance for two weeks because I played Pig instead of listening to Mr. Peabody. And I still have to go to class next Monday. I hate that school more than ever."

"I do not know what is the matter with you, Ricky Torres," I said. "I am sorry you lost your allowance. But I do not see why you can't go to class and learn some manners. If you did, you would not be in this trouble."

I was fuming mad. The boys were ruining Mr. Peabody's school. Every week I got dressed up for nothing. If the boys were not going to be gentlemen, how could we be true lovely ladies?

Wait! I had an idea.

"Good morning, class," said Ms. Colman.

"Good morning, Ms. Colman!" I said. (I love Ms. Colman. She is a wonderful teacher. And a lovely lady besides.)

"Everyone, please find your seats now. It is time to take attendance," said Ms. Colman.

I wished I could move to a different seat. Ricky, Natalie, and I sit together in the front row because we wear glasses. But I did not feel like sitting next to Ricky that morning.

I wanted to sit next to Hannie and Nancy so I could tell them my plan. (Hannie and Nancy sit at the back of the room together. I used to sit with them before I got my glasses.)

"Karen? Would you please answer when I call your name?" said Ms. Colman.

"Sorry. I am here," I answered. (I used my indoor voice. That is the one Ms. Colman likes.)

I thought about my plan. I was going to have a tea party. It was going to be very fancy. And it was going to be *for girls only*. That way we could get dressed up and put on our best manners for *real*.

Let's see, I thought. I will have the party at the big house. I will use my flowery china tea set. I will mail invitations. I will make delicious things to eat. . . .

I could hardly wait to get started.

# The Pudding Mess

Nancy came to my house to play after school.

"Want to cook something?" I asked. "I just love to cook." (I did not say anything about the rice mess or the cookie mess.)

"Okay," said Nancy. "What should we make?"

"Mommy bought butterscotch pudding mix yesterday. Let's ask if we can make that," I suggested.

Mommy said we could make the pudding. "But I will stay in the kitchen in case you need me," she said.

"Do not say anything unless we ask. Okay?" I said.

"Okay," agreed Mommy.

Nancy and I read the directions on the box. All we had to do was put the pudding mix into a pan with two cups of milk. Then cook and stir the pudding until it boiled.

Nancy and I each measured one cup of milk. We took turns pouring in half the package of pudding mix.

"You know what we should put in now?" I said. "Raisins. And cinnamon. That would be so delicious!"

"Shouldn't we just follow the recipe?" asked Nancy.

"Ahem," coughed Mommy. (I could tell she wanted to say something even though I did not ask.)

"Mom-my. We can make it by ourselves," I said.

"All right," said Mommy. "I am sorry."

"Trust me," I said to Nancy. "This will

be great. Here, you put in the raisins. I'll put in the cinnamon."

"How many raisins?" asked Nancy.

"Oh, a couple of handfuls should do it," I said.

Nancy dropped in two handfuls of raisins.

It was time for the cinnamon. I opened the top and shook the can.

Uh-oh. I had opened the wrong part of the can. It was the part with the great big hole. Heaps of cinnamon poured in. I was so surprised, I dropped the can into the pot. The pot tipped over.

"Oh, no!" Nancy and I cried.

Pudding mix and cinnamon and raisins sloshed over the stove and dripped onto the floor. It was a pudding mess!

Rice mess. Cookie mess. Pudding mess! I was so mad. I could tell Nancy was, too.

Mommy was very nice. She did not say anything. She just handed us some towels to clean up the mess.

Then she gave us cookies and juice. (We

had used up the milk in the pudding.)

By the time we finished eating, I felt much better.

"Mommy, may I call Daddy? I want to ask him about my tea party," I said. (I had already told Mommy my plan to have a *real* tea party at the big house.)

"All right. But remember, Daddy is at work. Do not keep him on the phone too long," said Mommy.

I called Daddy and asked him really fast about the tea party. He said I could have one. Hurray!

"Let's make the invitations," I said to Nancy. "We can draw teapots and teacups on them. They will be beautiful."

"Who should we invite?" asked Nancy.

"Let's invite *all* the girls in our class," I said. "We want it to be a big, fancy tea party."

"Even Pamela?" asked Nancy.

"Yes. She thinks the boys are being dumb, too," I replied. "We will tell everyone to get really dressed up. Even dressier than we do for Mr. Peabody's school."

"Wow!" said Nancy.

"I will make brownies." (I decided I still loved to cook.) "I will cut them up small and put them on doilies. It will be perfect for lovely, lovely ladies," I said.

We worked hard the rest of the afternoon. By the time Nancy had to leave, we had made all the invitations we needed.

**15**

# The Tea Party War

"This is so great!" I said. "Everyone I invited is coming to the tea party on Saturday."

It was Monday. I was at school with Hannie and Nancy. We were on the playground. I was talking very loudly. That's because Ricky and some other boys were standing nearby. I wanted to make sure they could hear me.

"I am glad no boys are invited," said Hannie in her loudest voice. "They would ruin everything. Just like they ruined Mr. Peabody's class."

That did it. A few of the boys came over, including Ricky.

"We don't care about going to your dumb tea party anyway," he said.

"Oh, really?" I replied. "We are having brownies. We are going to get dressed up. And we are going to have *fun!*"

"It's going to be so great," added Leslie.

"It will be great without boys around to spoil everything," said Pamela. "Boys have no manners. That is why they are *not* invited."

"Come on," said Bobby. "Let's go play ball. All this talk about tea parties is hurting my ears."

I did not say one word to Ricky the rest of the afternoon. So I was surprised when he came over to me later at Mr. Peabody's. He mumbled something that sounded like, "May I have this dance?"

Maybe he really does want to come to the tea party, I thought. Maybe he is trying to be nice. But maybe not. Maybe he said something dumb and I just did not hear him right.

"What did you say?" I asked. "I did not hear you."

Ricky's face changed. He frowned.

"MAY I HAVE THESE PANTS?" he said.

"No. Thank. You," I replied. I was mad at him again.

Hannie and Bobby were dancing next to us.

"Ow!" cried Hannie. "You stepped on my foot."

"I didn't mean it," said Bobby.

"I bet you did!" said Hannie.

"I didn't mean it before. But now I do," said Bobby. And he stepped on her foot again.

The boys and girls did not get along all afternoon. Or the next day at school, either.

"May I have this dance?" asked Hank in a high, silly voice.

"Yes, you may," answered Bobby. "But only if you have very good manners."

72

"I'll try," said Hank.

They started dancing together, the way girls do.

"Ow! You stepped on my toe. Now you cannot come to my tea party," said Hank.

"Oh, too bad," answered Bobby. "I love brownies. And getting all dressed up. And dancing the walrus."

The boys thought that was so, so funny. They were acting dumber than ever.

# Karen's Perfect Brownies

" 'Bye, Mommy! See you Sunday," I called.

It was dinnertime on Friday. I ran across the lawn to the big house with Andrew. We were late because I had been looking for my new hair clip at Mommy's house. I had to have it for my tea party on Saturday.

"Hi, kids," said Daddy. "Come join us in the kitchen. Dinner is on the table."

"Hi, everyone!" I cried.

"Hi!" said Elizabeth, Kristy, Sam, Charlie, Nannie, and Emily Michelle. (David Michael did not say anything.)

For dinner, we were having pot roast, rice, and string beans. The rice looked dry and fluffy, just the way it is supposed to. That is because Nannie made it.

When we finished eating, we cleaned up the kitchen together. I helped Nannie load the dishwasher.

"Nannie," I said, "tomorrow is my tea party. I want to make brownies tonight."

"How about letting me help you? Brownies can be a little complicated," said Nannie.

I liked to cook by myself. But I had not been doing very well lately. And the brownies had to be right.

"Okay," I said. "We will make them together."

Soon Nannie and I were alone in the kitchen. We found a cookbook and opened it to the brownie recipe.

"I always start by lining up my ingredients," said Nannie.

Here is what we needed: 2 squares of unsweetened chocolate, ⅓ cup butter, ⅔ cup flour, ½ tsp baking powder, ¼ tsp salt, 2 eggs, 1 cup sugar, 1 tsp vanilla.

There was that secret code again. *Tsp.* But guess what. Nannie knew what it meant.

"*Tsp* stands for *teaspoon,*" she said. "When you come to something you don't understand, just ask."

The first thing we had to do was melt the chocolate and butter in a pan.

"Let's turn the fire way up, Nannie," I said. "The butter will melt faster that way."

"Fast is not always best," Nannie replied. "It is important to read and *follow* the directions."

The directions said we should use very low heat. So we did.

Next, we had to mix up all the dry things. Flour, sugar, baking powder, and salt.

Then Nannie let me beat the eggs.

"You never did anything bad, eggs. I am sorry I have to beat you," I said. (Nannie thought that was a funny joke.)

We mixed everything together. I got some batter on my fingers and tasted it. Yum!

The last thing we had to do was pour the batter into a pan and bake it for half an hour.

While we waited, I told Nannie about Mr. Peabody's school. I told her how dumb the boys were acting.

"They do not have any manners at all!" I said.

"Maybe the boys do not like getting dressed up and having to act a certain way," said Nannie. "But they have good manners most of the time, don't they? After all, manners are really ways to be considerate of other people's feelings."

"I guess," I said. "But I'm still glad the boys are not coming to my tea party."

There were ten minutes left on the timer. I walked up to Nannie, looked her in the eye, and said, "May I have this dance?"

Nannie smiled. "Yes, you may," she answered. (Nannie has very good manners.)

I hummed the skating song and waltzed around the kitchen with Nannie. *One*, two, three. *One*, two, three.

*Ding!* The timer went off. Our brownies were ready.

I looked at them sitting in the pan. They were not burnt. They were not soupy. They were perfect.

"Cool, Nannie! I am a good cook," I said. "And you are the best teacher!"

# Party Dress

"Time for me to get ready, Moosie!" I said.

It was Saturday. The day of my tea party. I was gigundoly excited.

I was going to wear my special party dress. And my new hair clip. But how should I fix my hair?

I stood in front of the mirror. Maybe I should have gone to the beauty parlor. Lovely ladies always have their hair done before their tea parties. But I had my hair cut at Gloriana's House of Hair once, and

I was practically bald when I came out.

I pulled my hair back in a ponytail. No. I wear it that way all the time.

Pigtails? No. I only had one hair clip.

Then I did something Kristy does sometimes. I pulled half my hair back in a ponytail and let the rest hang down. That was it. I looked pretty. And very grown-up.

My feet were next. I was wearing my nice black party shoes. I liked them a lot. But which socks?

First I tried pink. They looked okay. Then I tried white. They looked okay. Then I tried blue. Oh, no. They looked good, too!

I was tired of putting on and taking off my socks. So I just left the blue ones on.

What else did I need? I did not have a hat. Or a fancy umbrella. Too bad. But I did not really need them since I wasn't going out of the house.

I did have my white gloves, though. Gloves are very important for lovely ladies.

*Knock, knock.*

80

"May I come in?" said Kristy, peeking into my room. "I brought you something."

Kristy was holding a white straw pocketbook. It was the one she used when she had to get dressed up.

"Oh, Kristy, thank you!" I cried.

"I put a handkerchief, some mints, and a comb in it," said Kristy.

I held it up in front of the mirror. Kristy and I both started to laugh. My hair was perfect. I was wearing my socks and my shoes. I was holding Kristy's pocketbook. But I was still in my underwear! I had been saving my dress for last.

Kristy helped me put it on. Then we went downstairs.

Elizabeth had already spread a white tablecloth on the dining room table.

I set out my flowery china, real linen napkins, and silver candlesticks with two tall white candles. (I wasn't allowed to light them, but they looked pretty anyway.)

Daddy always buys flowers for the living room on the weekend. He said I could borrow them for my tea party. I set the vase in the middle of the table between the candles.

"Karen, that looks beautiful," said Kristy.

The last thing was the food: cookies from the store, cinnamon toast with the crusts cut off, chamomile tea that Nannie made, and the perfect brownies.

The night before, Nannie had shown me how to put the food in pretty rows on plates.

"It's the little touches that make the difference," she said.

*Ding-dong!*

I raced to the door. Hannie and Melody were there.

"Hi!" I cried.

Nancy and a few other girls were coming up the walk behind them. My tea party was starting!

# Here Come the Boys!

**W**ow! My guests looked beautiful. I had never seen so many flowered dresses, straw hats, Mary Janes, ballet slippers, bows, ribbons, and fancy hair clips in one room.

"It was so very kind of you to invite me today, Karen," said Natalie.

"My pleasure, I am sure," I answered. "Won't you come into the dining room and have a cup of tea?"

"I would be delighted."

Kristy had promised to be the waitress. She was passing around the food and helping to pour the tea.

"This toast is simply scrumptious," said Hannie.

"How pleasant of you to say so," I replied. "You have very good manners."

"I got them at Mr. Peabody's school," said Hannie.

"Ah, yes," said Nancy. "I plan to attend next year."

"Oh, you must. I have learned so much already," said Natalie. She took a sip of tea. She made sure to hold her pinky away from the cup.

Melody was sitting by herself. Her ankles were crossed and her hands were folded in her lap. Melody did not know anyone except me, Hannie, and Nancy. That is because she is new in the neighborhood and goes to a different school.

"You are sitting so nicely," I said to her.

(I remembered that it is good manners to begin a conversation with a compliment.)

"Thank you," said Melody. "I went to Miss Labonne's School of Manners before I moved here."

"Well, it certainly shows," I said. "Please let me pour you a cup of tea and introduce you to some of the other guests."

"Thank you," said Melody. "Your manners are divine."

*Ding-dong!*

"I'll get it," said Kristy. "You stay here and see to your guests."

I wondered who could be at the door. Everyone I invited was already at the party. Then I heard Kristy talking much louder than she usually does.

"I really don't think you should go in there," she said.

I turned to the doorway. I saw Kristy's back. She was holding out her arms, trying to block . . .

David Michael! He was not supposed to

be here. And half the boys in Ms. Colman's class were with him. What did they think they were doing?

"We are here to crash the tea party," announced Ricky.

# The Bad-News Boys

Oh, no, I thought. This is bad news. But I am still going to behave like a lovely lady. (Do lovely ladies get gigundoly mad?)

"Excuse me, Kristy," I said. "May I talk to you, please? Over here?"

Kristy followed me to a corner of the room.

"What are we going to do?" I moaned. "We cannot be truly lovely ladies with these boys around. That is why we did not invite them in the first place."

"I know, Karen. I am sorry," Kristy replied.

"Just look at them. They're a grubby mess," I said.

The boys were wearing jeans and sloppy shirts with the tails hanging out. They had on old sneakers and baseball caps. And none of them looked very clean.

I sighed. First the boys ruined Mr. Peabody's class. Now they were going to ruin my party.

"Kristy, please make them go home," I whispered.

"All right, boys," said Kristy. "You have crashed the party. Now it's time to go."

Some of the boys turned to leave. But David Michael seemed to be in charge.

"We are staying," he said.

Darn old David Michael. We had hardly talked to each other since we started going to Mr. Peabody's school. He acted like it was my fault he had to go. Just because I liked it and he didn't.

And I think he was mad because I left

him out of the tea party. Couldn't he see it was for *girls?*

I gave David Michael a dirty look. But that did not stop him.

"It is my dining room, too," he said. He went to the other room to get more chairs.

"I'm sorry, Karen," whispered Kristy. "I think we will have to let the boys stay."

"All right," I said. "But only because lovely ladies do not fight."

Kristy helped squeeze in more chairs. Soon the boys were sitting down and being served with the other guests.

"Hey, Karen. These brownies are good," said Ricky.

I could hardly believe it! Ricky had started a conversation with a compliment.

"Thank you," I replied. "I made them myself. Well, almost. Here, have another."

"Don't mind if I do," said Ricky.

I looked around the room. The boys were behaving much better than I had expected. They were not making animal noises. They were not throwing food. They were not burping. They were not even making fun of us.

I think they really wanted to be at my party. And I think they wanted to have a good time.

"Hello, Hank," I said. "Would you like another piece of toast?" (Hank likes to eat a lot.)

"I don't want to make a pig of myself," said Hank.

"You are not a pig," I told him. "As long as you don't snort."

We spent the rest of the afternoon talking, laughing, eating, and drinking tea. It was one of the nicest tea parties I ever had. I was sorry when it was over.

"Good-bye. I am glad you came to my party," I said to Bobby. Bobby can be a bully sometimes. But he did not do one mean thing all afternoon.

Before he left, Ricky helped me bring the teacups into the kitchen.

"This party was fun, Karen. Thanks," he said.

"Thank you for being such a good guest," I replied.

I really meant it.

# One, Two, Three

"**W**elcome everyone," said Mr. Peabody.

It was another Monday at Mr. Peabody's school. I could see the boys were going to behave better this time. Just as they did at my tea party.

Well, some of the boys at least. Most of them were still glued to the wall. But Ricky and Bobby and Hank had actually said hi when they came in.

"We will begin today's class with a review of the lindy," said Mr. Peabody. "Martin?"

Martin bowed and began to play.

I saw Ricky coming toward me. But the nice boy I had danced with before reached me first. Awesome!

"May I have this dance?" he said.

"Yes, you may," I replied.

Toe, heel. Toe, heel. Step. Step. Toe, heel. Toe, heel. Step. Step.

After the lindy, we learned a dance called the cha-cha. I saw Daddy and Elizabeth do the cha-cha once in our living room. It looked like fun.

Mr. and Mrs. Peabody showed us the steps.

"One, two, cha-cha-cha. Three, four, cha-cha-cha. Watch my feet, cha-cha-cha," called Mr. Peabody.

We followed along. Then it was time to dance with partners.

Even before the music started, Ricky began to run in my direction. I held my breath. I hoped he would not say, "May I have these pants?"

He didn't!

"May I have this dance?" he asked.

"Charmed, I'm sure!" I replied.

Martin played a really good cha-cha song. Mr. Peabody called out the steps, "One, two, cha-cha-cha. Three, four, cha-cha-cha."

I felt like a truly lovely lady. I was wearing my beautiful party dress. I was wearing my white gloves. And I was dancing with my smiling pretend husband.

I closed my eyes. I felt like a princess dancing at the palace ball. (I wondered if Cinderella knew the cha-cha.)

When the dance was over, Mr. Peabody said, "Everyone stay right where you are. We are going to play a game."

Oh, goody! I love games. I especially love to win.

"I want you and your partner to look around the room and try to guess how many tiles are on our beautiful dance-room floor. When I point to you, call out your number," said Mr. Peabody.

Ricky and I looked around the room. Then we whispered our numbers to each other. We agreed on a number in the middle.

When Mr. Peabody pointed to us, we called out together, "Two hundred and twenty-five!"

Guess what! The right number was two hundred and fifty. The number we picked was the closest. So we won. We each got a dinosaur eraser for a prize.

"Karen and Ricky, will you now lead us in a waltz?" said Mr. Peabody.

I was so excited! Mr. and Mrs. Peabody were usually the leaders. Now Ricky and I would be. Everyone turned to look at us.

"Martin?" said Mr. Peabody.

Martin bowed and began to play.

Ricky was blushing a little. But I could tell he was not going to do anything silly.

"May I have this dance?" he asked.

"Yes, you may," I replied.

Ricky and I waltzed around and around the room, counting together, *one*, two, three, *one*, two, three.

And our dance was just the way I had always dreamed it would be.

## About the Author

ANN M. MARTIN lives in New York City and loves animals, especially cats. She has two cats of her own, Mouse and Rosie.

Other books by Ann M. Martin that you might enjoy are *Stage Fright*; *Me and Katie (the Pest)*; and the books in *The Baby-sitters Club* series.

Ann likes ice cream and *I Love Lucy*. And she has her own little sister, whose name is Jane.

## Little Sister

Don't miss #29

### KAREN'S CARTWHEEL

"Karen? Karen?"

I shook my head. Natalie Springer was tugging at my elbow.

"Yeah?"

"We are supposed to be working on our floor routines," said Natalie. "Miss Donovan told me to be your partner. Come on."

Natalie and I practiced and practiced. It is a good thing Miss Donovan puts mats on the floor. Natalie falls a lot.

But not me. I did not start falling until Miss Donovan added a cartwheel to my routine. Then, flip-flop. I was on my bottom more than I was on my hands or my feet.

Those darn old cartwheels!

102

## Little Sister

by Ann M. Martin
author of The Baby-sitters Club®

*More Titles...* ➡